When crew members watched for icebergs, they looked for telltale signs such as:

**Ice Blink:** white light created by sunlight or moonlight reflecting off ice

**White Foam:** foam made by waves crashing into icebergs

**Growlers:** small chunks of ice that may have broken off larger icebergs

## Watching for Ice

Even higher than the bridge, at the top of the ship, was the crow's nest. Two lookouts stood there on each watch. They looked for icebergs, ships, and other hazards. The lookouts on *Titanic* used only their eyes. They did not have binoculars to help them watch for icebergs. At that time, lookouts rarely used binoculars. Additionally, the crew kept *Titanic*'s binoculars in a locker. An officer who went to work on a different ship took the key to the locker with him.

*Titanic's binoculars keys*

**bridge**—the control center of a ship

A photograph taken after the sinking shows 13 of *Titanic*'s 18 surviving stewardesses.

## Caring for Guests

During the voyage stewards and stewardesses worked long hours to ensure the comfort of their passengers. They carried bags, made beds, cleaned rooms, and helped serve meals. They were ready to answer any time a passenger called or rang a bell.

Although crew members worked on a beautiful ship, they did not often get the chance to enjoy the voyage. They worked up to 16 hours a day. In the evening they might have time for a walk on deck or a game of cards. They did not get a day off until the voyage ended.

A steward's white jacket was recovered from *Titanic*'s wreckage on the ocean floor.

## CRAMPED QUARTERS

Up to eight stewards and stewardesses shared one room, which was often uncomfortable and lacked privacy. However, the crew's quarters on *Titanic* were better than the crew rooms on other ships. Ship designer Thomas Andrews asked for crew members' input when he designed the ship. Stewardess Violet Jessup noted her bunk was positioned in the way she had suggested, which gave her more privacy.

# Feeding the Passengers

Cooks and dining room staff made sure passengers were well fed. Bakers worked through the night to bake bread for the next day. Pastry cooks and assistants made desserts. Other cooks made main courses.

In the first-class dining room, saloon stewards in dark suits took meal orders. They served meals such as lamb with mint sauce and roasted duckling with applesauce. Saloon stewards also served second- and third-class passengers.

Eating in *Titanic's* first-class dining room was like dining in a fancy restaurant.

# Titanic's Pantry

**flour:** 200 barrels

**butter:** 6,000 pounds (2,722 kilograms)

**eggs:** 40,000

**green peas:** 2,250 pounds (1,021 kg)

**meat:** 75,000 pounds (34,019 kg)

**milk:** 1,500 gallons (5,678 liters)

**ice cream:** 1,750 quarts (1,656 L)

**jams:** 1,120 pounds (508 kg)

**lemons:** 16,000

**lettuce:** 7,000 heads

**oranges:** 36,000

**potatoes:** 40 tons (36 metric tons)

**sugar:** 10,000 pounds (4,356 kg)

# Sweating in the Boiler Rooms

Trimmers, firemen, and pushers worked day and night to stoke the boilers that powered the ship's engines. The boiler rooms were brutally hot. The workers' gray flannel shirts were dripping with sweat by the time their shifts ended. Black coal dust covered the workers' faces.

**Pushers:** The pushers made sure coal burned as hot as possible and steam pressure in the engines was suitable. If a furnace needed more coal, pushers signaled to others by hitting the floor with a shovel.

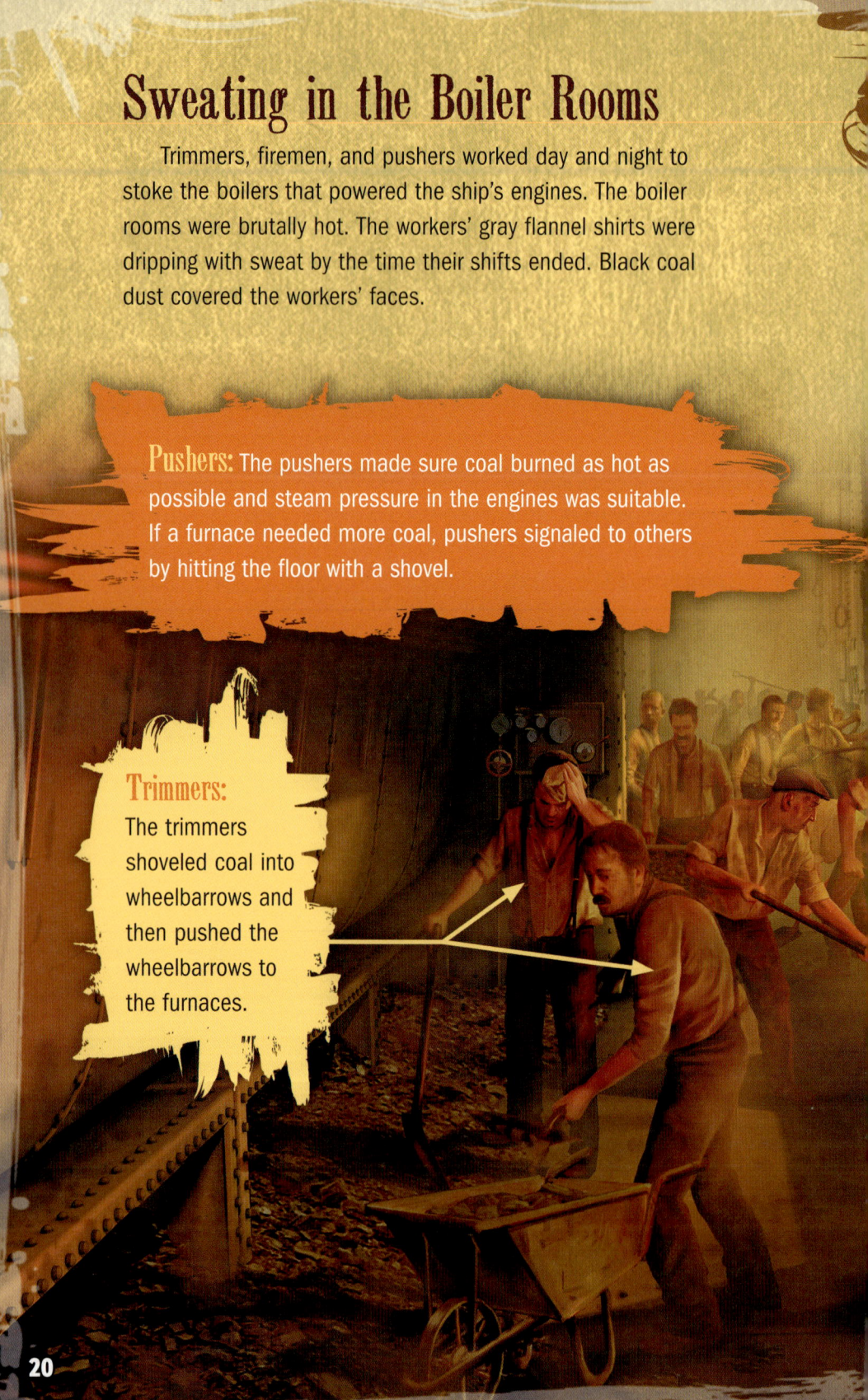

**Trimmers:** The trimmers shoveled coal into wheelbarrows and then pushed the wheelbarrows to the furnaces.

**FACT:** The firemen had their own mess hall on the third deck of the ship. Usually they ate "oodle." This was a soup made of beef, carrots, and onions.

**Firemen:** The firemen shoveled coal into a furnace and reached into the furnace with a long tool to loosen and scrape out **clinkers**. They also raked ashes in the furnace.

clinker—the part of coal that does not burn

Passengers exercise on cycle racing machines in *Titanic*'s gymnasium.

## Making Music

At dinner and teatime, the ship's eight musicians entertained first-class passengers. Five of them gave concerts in a lounge after dinner. A pianist, cellist, and violinist played French melodies in a reception room outside the ship's fancy restaurants. The musicians also played during the Sunday morning church service.

**FACT:** The musicians did not room with other crew members. Instead, they traveled as passengers and stayed in second-class cabins.

# First-Class Luxury

Some people working on *Titanic* helped and entertained first-class passengers while the ship was at sea.

★ An instructor showed first-class passengers how to use the exercise equipment in the ship's gym.

★ A squash pro gave lessons on the game, which is similar to racquetball.

★ In the library a steward loaned out books.

★ Three male stewards and two female stewardesses worked in the Turkish baths, a type of spa, on the ship's lower decks. The stewards cared for first-class passengers who wanted to use the steam room, cooling room, and shampooing room.

the cooling room of *Titanic*'s Turkish baths

# Mail Call

Letters and packages shipped from Great Britain and Ireland to the United States were an important part of *Titanic*'s cargo. *Titanic* was a Royal Mail Ship, which is why it was known as the RMS *Titanic*. The ship had five postal workers. Three were from the United States and two were British. The ship carried more than 7 million pieces of mail. The workers would spend the entire voyage sorting mail. The postal workers sorted more than 60,000 letters each day.

Workers in Ireland loaded mail onto *Titanic* before it headed out to sea.

This letter was written by *Titanic*'s band leader, Wallace Hartley, while onboard the ship.

On board R.M.S. "TITANIC"
Wednesday 191

My dear parents —

Just a line to say we have got away all right. It's been a bit of a rush but I am just getting a little settled. This is a fine ship & there ought to be plenty of money on her. I've missed sending love post... it would ... to have ... if only for ... but I ... ge it. ... ne band ... em very nice ... to buy some ... y washing ... post. ... arrive home on the Sunday morning. We are due here on the Saturday. I'm glad mother's foot is better. With love to all

Wallace

**FACT:** The postal workers were expected to give their lives to protect the mail if necessary. All five postal workers on *Titanic* worked to try to save the mail as the ship was sinking. None survived.

# Messages from *Titanic*'s Passengers

Jack Phillips

"Hello Boy. Dining with you tonight in spirit, heart with you always. Best love, Girl."

"No sickness. All well."

"Fine voyage, fine ship."

## Staying in Touch

Radio operators Jack Phillips and Harold Bride kept the ship in touch with the outside world. They used a Marconi wireless set to send and receive messages in **Morse code**. An antenna on *Titanic* broadcast the messages. Other antennas on shore or on other ships picked up the messages.

The men also kept the radio equipment working. On the night of April 12, *Titanic*'s radio broke. Phillips and Bride spent that night and the next morning fixing the radio. They then got back to work sending and decoding messages. Phillips and Bride worked on the boat deck, the same deck the bridge was on.

After *Titanic* struck the iceberg on April 14, 1912, the ship's radio operators sent the telegraph message below to *Olympic*. The message told *Olympic*'s crew that *Titanic* had struck an iceberg and provided the sinking ship's coordinates.

The Marconi International Marine Communication Co., Ltd.,
WATERGATE HOUSE, YORK BUILDINGS, ADELPHI, LONDON, W.C.

No. "OLYMPIC"   OFFICE   14 Apr   19 12
                         CHARGES TO PAY.

Handed in at TITANIC

                                   Total

To  OLYMPIC

Eleven pm NEW YORK TIME TITANIC SENDING OUT SIGNALS OF DISTRESS ANSWERED HIS CALLS.
TITANIC REPLIES AND GIVES ME HIS POSITION 41.46 N 50 14 W AND SAYS "WE HAVE STRUCK AN ICE BERG".

**Sleeping Quarters:**
The two Marconi operators shared a cabin next to the rooms they worked in. When one worked, the other had a break. They worked day and night for six hours at a time.

**The Marconi Room:**
The radio operators sat at a workstation and wore a headset to hear the signals. They used a key to tap messages in Morse code. Messages came in through receiving equipment.

**The Silent Room:**
Circuits turned electrical current into radio signals. The signals were sent out through an antenna on top of the ship.

Harold Bride works in Titanic's Marconi room.

a replica of a Marconi set similar to the one Titanic used

**Morse code**—a method of sending messages by radio using a series of long and short clicks

CHAPTER 3
# All Hands on Deck

## Warnings

Sunday, April 14, 1912, dawned bright and clear. It was a normal, busy day at sea for *Titanic*'s crew members. In the radio room, Phillips and Bride worked through a backlog of messages passengers wanted to send to shore.

The men also received messages from other ships warning of ice in the area. They delivered some of these reports to the officers, but the officers showed little concern. *Titanic* was not sailing near the reported areas of ice.

The night of April 14 was perfectly clear and calm in the North Atlantic. This made it difficult for *Titanic*'s lookouts to spot waves breaking at the bases of icebergs.

That evening, however, Phillips received another message warning of ice. It stated there was an ice field near the ship. However, Phillips did not realize the importance of the message. He did not deliver the warning to officers on the bridge.

*Mesaba*

## ICE MESSAGES TO *TITANIC*

**9:00 A.M.**
*Caronia* sends a message warning of icebergs and growlers.

**1:42 P.M.**
*Baltic* warns another ship saw "icebergs and large quantities of field ice."

**9:40 P.M.**
*Mesaba* says it "saw much heavy pack ice and great number large icebergs."

**10:50 P.M.**
*Californian* notifies *Titanic* it is "stopped and surrounded by ice."

*Californian*

Frederick Fleet

## Impact

Lookouts Frederick Fleet and Reginald Lee had icebergs on their minds when they began their shift in the crow's nest on April 14. It was a cold, calm evening, and the lack of wind made spotting an iceberg difficult.

At 11:40 p.m., Fleet saw an object in the distance. An iceberg was about 500 yards (460 m) in front of the ship. He called the bridge, and the officer immediately ordered the quartermaster to turn the ship. The officer also signaled the engine room to reverse the engines. The plan was to move the ship to the left to avoid hitting the iceberg.

However, the order came too late. The ship could not make the sharp turn. The iceberg scraped against *Titanic*, gashing its side.

**FACT:** Less than a minute passed between the time the lookouts spotted the iceberg and *Titanic*'s collision with it.

Workers tried to escape one of *Titanic*'s boiler rooms as it rapidly filled with water.

## Trouble Down Below

People immediately felt the effect of the collision in the lower decks at the front of the ship. The mailroom began to flood as water burst in. Postal workers quickly carried mailbags to the sorting room above. Soon the mailroom was too flooded for them to go back inside.

In a flooding boiler room, firemen quickly shut down the furnaces. As leading fireman Frederick Barrett gave the order to close them down, water rushed into the room. He quickly jumped to the next boiler room as the watertight door closed behind him.

**FACT:** Some experts think *Titanic* would not have sunk if it had hit the iceberg head-on. The front of the ship was sturdier than the side. Therefore, if the front of the ship had hit the iceberg, it may have crumpled but not ripped open. Other historians argue the ship would have sunk anyway.

The boiler rooms and mailroom were some of the first rooms to fill with water.

# Calling the Crew

On deck Captain Smith received reports of the damage and knew the ship was in danger. When the iceberg gashed the side of the ship, six of its 16 watertight compartments toward the bow began filling with water. Thomas Andrews, the ship's designer, was onboard. He informed Smith that *Titanic*'s bow could not stay afloat with that much water in it. As the bow sank lower, water would spill into the other compartments. Andrews accurately estimated the ship would sink within two hours. At 12:05 a.m. on April 15, Smith gave the order to uncover the lifeboats. When the boats were ready, he told crew members to start loading women and children into them.

Smith ordered Bride and Phillips to radio distress signals to anyone nearby. Crew members launched bright flares into the sky to attract the attention of nearby ships. The call for "all hands on deck" was passed around the ship. The boatswain, able seamen, and other crew members went on deck to help with the lifeboats. Some stewards and stewardesses went below deck to tell passengers to go to the ship's deck. Others walked around the deck instructing passengers to put on their life vests.

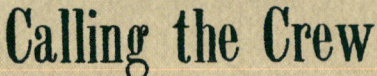

One of *Titanic*'s cork-filled life vests was recovered off the Canadian coast after the sinking.

Stewardesses encouraged passengers to put on their life vests and make their way to the lifeboats.

> " We did not think then there was anything serious. The general idea of the crew was that we were going to get the boats ready in case of emergency, and the sooner we got the job done the quicker we should get below again. "
>
> —able seaman Joseph Scarrott

# Chapter 4
# Tragedy and Rescue

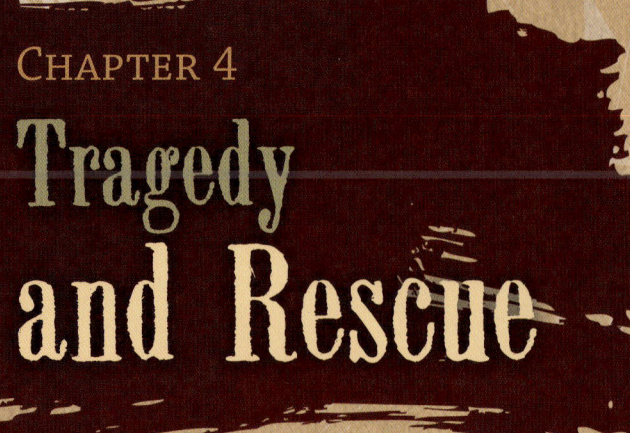

## Into the Lifeboats

The engines had been shut down, and steam being released from the boilers whistled through the valves on deck. This created a noisy roar as the crew uncovered the lifeboats. It was so loud that Second Officer Charles Herbert Lightoller had to use hand signals to tell crew members to get the boats into place. The noise died down as the first boats were ready to lower into the water. Lightoller and other crew members began helping women and children enter the boats.

### Lifeboat Types
**Total Lifeboats: 20**

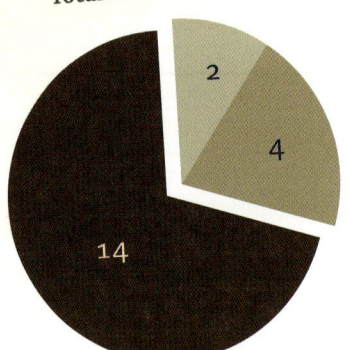

### Lifeboat Capacities
**Total Lifeboat Capacity: 1,178**

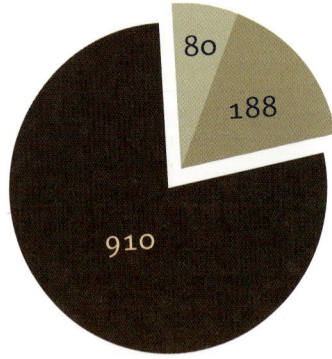

- Wooden Cutters
- Collapsible Lifeboats*
- Wooden Lifeboats

*Two collapsible lifeboats were not launched correctly. They were washed off the ship as it sank; about 60 people swam to these boats and were saved.

As they realized the large ship was sinking, crew members filled the lifeboats with as many people as they could.

Total passengers on *Titanic*: 2,200
Lifeboat capacity: 1,178
Survivors: 712

At first it was not easy for crew members to convince people to get into the lifeboats. They had to lower the boats 60 feet (18 m) from the deck to the water. Passengers thought it was safer to stay on the large ship. Also some crew members feared the **davits** holding the lifeboats would break if the boats were full. Additionally, the general confusion on deck and rush to launch the lifeboats likely prevented crew members from filling them to capacity. Investigations into the sinking suggest that more than 450 additional people may have survived if the lifeboats had been filled to capacity.

*davit*—a small crane used on ships

Titanic's musicians played through the panic on deck as the sinking ship began to tilt.

# Working to the End

As the crew loaded the lifeboats, the ship's musicians played in an effort to keep passengers calm. At first they played in the first-class lounge. Later they moved to the lobby and boat deck. Survivors recalled the brave men playing happy music as the ship came ever closer to sinking. None of the musicians survived.

Crew members on the ship's lower levels did their best to keep *Titanic* afloat. Engineers used pumps to purge water from the ship. Firemen shut down boilers so they would not explode. In the radio room, the operators sent messages asking for help.

Officers tried to keep order as the crew filled the last lifeboats. As men worked to ready the final lifeboat, a wave washed over the deck. It swept people into the ocean as the bow disappeared under the water. A few people managed to climb aboard a collapsible lifeboat that had been washed off the deck, but hundreds of others were stranded in the icy water.

# The Captain's Last Minutes

No one knows how Captain Edward Smith spent his final moments. One surviving passenger said Smith was washed overboard and then swam back to the bridge. Others said he brought a baby to a lifeboat and then swam away. It is certain, however, that he did not survive.

Titanic's engineers worked to keep the ship's lights on as long as possible.

# Final Moments

Those in the lifeboats watched helplessly as *Titanic* slipped under the ocean's surface at approximately 2:20 a.m. Some crew members described the scene:

Radio operator Harold Bride said, "Smoke and sparks were rushing out of her funnels … The ship was gradually turning on her nose—just like a duck does that goes down for a dive."

Fireman Jack Podesta recalled, "There was once when she seemed to hang in the same place for a long time, so naturally we thought the watertight doors would hold her. Then all of a sudden, she swerved and her bow went under, her **stern** rose up in the air. Out went her lights and the rumbling noise was terrible."

Bride survived by swimming to one of *Titanic*'s collapsible lifeboats, but his injuries were so great he had to be carried off the rescue ship *Carpathia*.

Crew members and passengers watched from *Titanic*'s lifeboats as the great ship went down.

Second Officer Charles Herbert Lightoller said, "Lights on board the *Titanic* were still burning, and a wonderful spectacle she made ... Suddenly all lights went out and the huge bulk was left in black darkness."

Seaman George Moore remembered, "I saw the forward part of her go down, and it appeared to me as if she broke in half, and then the after part went. I can remember two explosions."

**stern**—the back end of a ship

# Seeking Survivors

Those in the lifeboats heard the cries of the people struggling to survive in the icy water. Most did not row back toward the survivors. Crew members and passengers were afraid of being swamped if others tried to climb aboard. However, Fifth Officer Harold Lowe and crew members in lifeboat 14 moved some of their passengers into other lifeboats. They then rowed back to pick up survivors.

Most of the people Lowe saw had died in the cold water. However, he found four people who were alive and also picked up passengers from a lifeboat that was sinking.

Many crew members remained committed to their jobs to the very end, giving their lives to save passengers and keep the ship functioning as long as possible. Of the 898 crew members who sailed on *Titanic*, 212 survived.

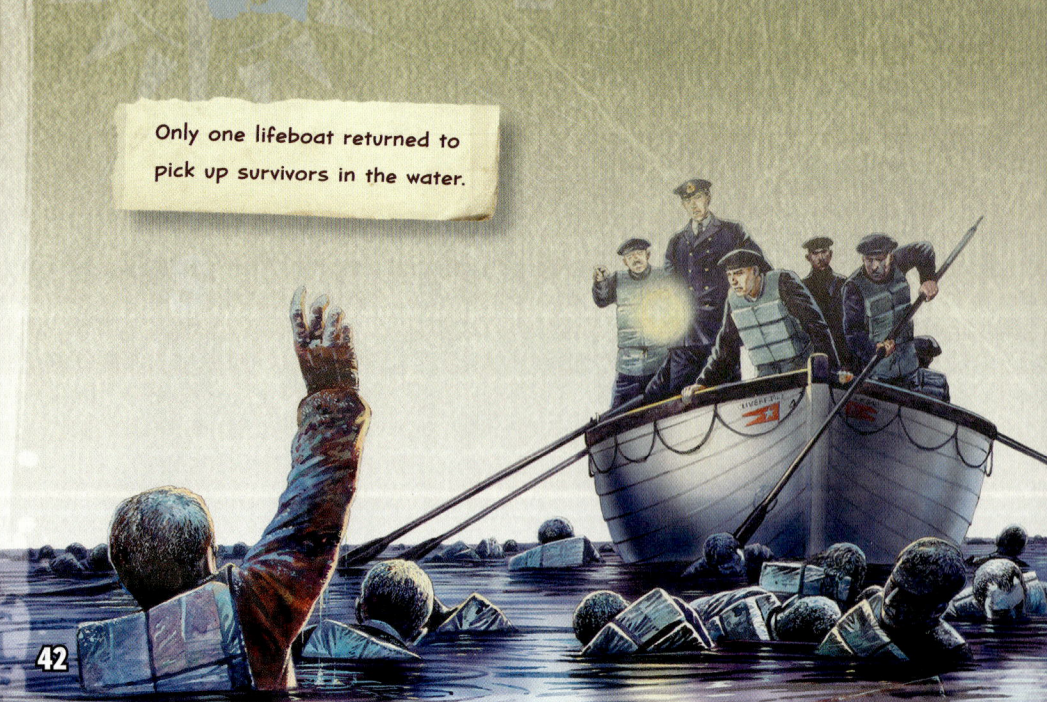

Only one lifeboat returned to pick up survivors in the water.

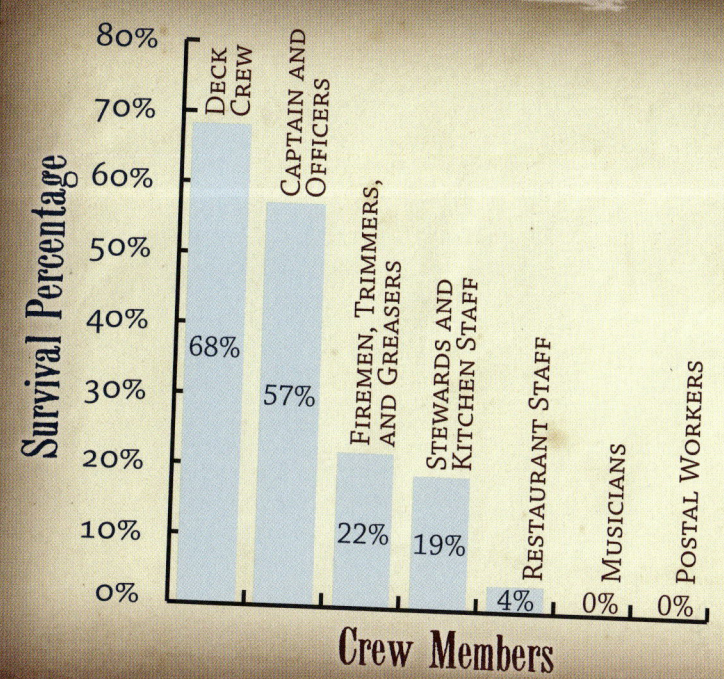

**Total Crew Survival Rates: 24 percent**
**Total Passenger Survival Rates: 38 percent**
**Total Survival Rate: 32 percent**

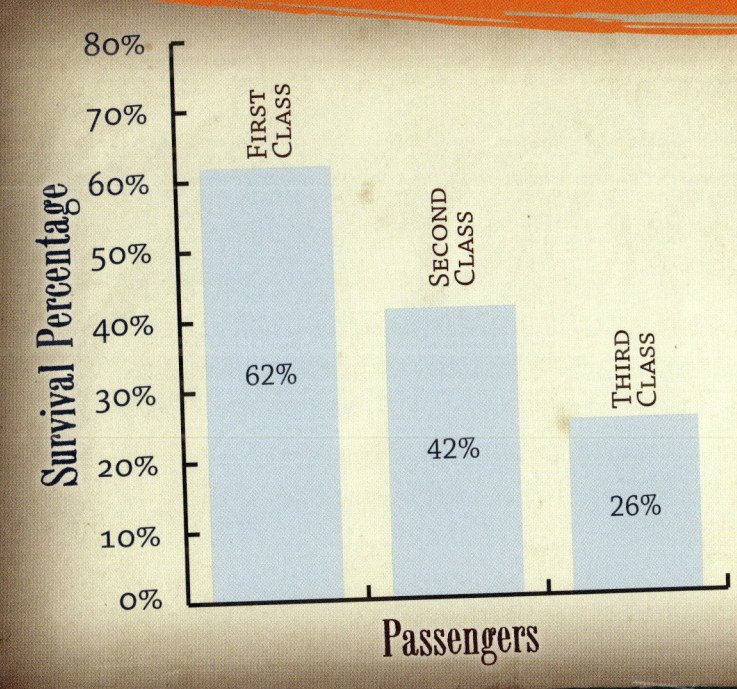

three stewards who survived the sinking

# Returning Home

At 4:00 a.m. on April 15, *Carpathia* arrived and picked up 712 survivors. The ship had received *Titanic*'s distress call. Radio operator Harold Bride helped send the names of survivors to shore.

The ship docked in New York on April 18. Some crew members went to the hospital to be treated for exposure to the cold. Others boarded another ship. *Lapland* took 167 crew members back to England on April 20. In most cases, the crew stopped being paid when *Titanic* sank. Many went back to work on another ship as soon as they could.

The crew members who were lost were not forgotten. Many had lived in Southampton, England. Memorials built there honor the hardworking men and women who lost their lives on *Titanic*.

# After Titanic

The *Titanic* disaster shocked the world. Committees formed in the United States and Great Britain to investigate the sinking. As a result of their investigations, several new **maritime** laws were passed. One called for all ships to be equipped with wireless communication devices and have an adequate number of operators. Another law formed the International Ice Patrol. This group would monitor the North Atlantic and share information about iceberg locations with ships. One of the most major changes involved lifeboat requirements. After *Titanic*'s sinking, ships were required to carry enough lifeboats for everyone onboard. Stricter rules were also put in place for how the crew members were trained to operate the lifeboats.

A memorial in Southampton honors the engineers who lost their lives on *Titanic* while trying to keep the ship's pumps working as long as possible.

**FACT:** Sidney Daniels was the last surviving *Titanic* crew member to die. He was 18 when he worked on the ship as a steward. He jumped off the sinking ship and climbed on an upside-down lifeboat that hadn't been launched properly. He died in 1983 at age 89.

**maritime**—related to the sea, ships, or sea travel

# Glossary

**backlog** (BAK-log)—a large amount of unfinished work

**bow** (BAU)—the front end of a ship

**bridge** (BRIJ)—the control center of a ship

**cargo** (KAHR-goh)—the goods carried by a ship, vehicle, or aircraft

**clinker** (KLING-kur)—the part of coal that does not burn

**crow's nest** (KROHZ NEST)—a lookout post located high above a ship

**davit** (DAHV-it)—a small crane used on ships

**lookout** (LUK-out)—a person who keeps watch for dangers from a high point with a 360° view

**maiden** (MAY-duhn)—first

**maritime** (MAR-ih-time)—related to the sea, ships, or sea travel

**Morse code** (MORSS KODE)—a method of sending messages by radio using a series of long and short clicks

**stern** (STERN)—the back end of a ship

**stoke** (STOHK)—to stir or add fuel to something that is burning

# Read More

**Lassieur, Allison.** *Can You Survive the Titanic?* You Choose: Survival. Mankato, Minn.: Capstone Press, 2012.

**Stewart, David.** *You Wouldn't Want to Sail on the Titanic!: One Voyage You'd Rather Not Make.* You Wouldn't Want to… New York: Franklin Watts, 2013.

**Zullo, Allan.** *Titanic: Young Survivors.* New York: Scholastic, 2012.

# Critical Thinking Using the Common Core

1. The chart on page 37 shows the total capacity of *Titanic*'s lifeboats and the number of survivors. Why are these numbers so different from one another? What factors limited crew members' abilities to load the lifeboats? Would the big drop into the ocean be intimidating? (Key Ideas and Details)
2. Pages 40 and 41 include quotes from different crew members describing *Titanic*'s sinking. How are these quotes similar to one another? How are they different? What might explain the differences? (Craft and Structure)
3. *Titanic* was built to be the most luxurious ship of its time. How did crew members' roles contribute to the luxury of *Titanic*? (Key Ideas and Details)

# Internet Sites

FactHound offers a safe, fun way to find Internet sites related to this book. All of the sites on FactHound have been researched by our staff.

Here's all you do:

Visit *www.facthound.com*

Type in this code: 9781491404201

# Index

able seamen, 10, 34, 35
Andrews, Thomas, 17, 34
assistant purser, 10
Barrett, Frederick, 32
boatswain, 10, 34
boiler room, 7, 11, 20-21, 32
Bride, Harold, 26, 28, 34, 40, 44
bridge, 14, 15, 29, 30, 39
*Carpathia*, 44
chief purser, 10
cooks, 7, 12, 18
crew members' nationalities, 7
Daniels, Sidney, 7, 45
elevators, 6, 12
engineers, 12, 14, 38
firemen, 12, 20, 21, 32, 38, 40, 43
first class, 18, 22-23, 38, 43
Fleet, Frederick, 4-5, 30
gym, 6, 23

icebergs, 4-5, 15, 29, 30, 31, 33, 34, 45
ice messages, 14, 28, 29
Ismay, Bruce, 8
Jessup, Violet, 17
*Lapland*, 44
Lee, Reginald, 4, 30
library, 23
lifeboats, 34, 35, 36-37, 38, 39, 40, 42, 45
life vests, 34
Lightoller, Charles Herbert, 9, 10, 36, 41
lookouts, 4-5, 15, 30
Lowe, Harold, 9, 42
luxury, 6, 22-23
mail, 24, 25, 32
Marconi system, 26-27
memorials, 44
Moore, George, 41
Morse code, 26, 27
musicians, 6, 22, 23, 38, 43
officers, 4-5, 8, 9, 10, 11, 12, 14, 15, 28-29, 30, 36, 38, 41, 42, 43

Phillips, Jack, 26, 28-29, 34
Podesta, Jack, 40
postal workers, 7, 24, 25, 32, 43
pushers, 20
quartermaster, 10, 14, 30
Scarrott, Joseph, 35
seamen, 7, 10, 41
second class, 18, 22, 43
Smith, Captain Edward, 8, 10, 12, 14, 34, 39, 43
Southampton, 7, 44
squash, 23
stewardesses, 12, 13, 16, 17, 23, 34
stewards, 7, 12, 16, 17, 18, 23, 34, 43, 45
survivors, 36, 37, 38, 39, 42, 43, 44, 45
third class, 7, 18, 43
trimmers, 20, 43
Turkish baths, 23
White Star Line, 7, 8

# The Titanic's Crew

## Working Aboard the Great Ship

by Terri Dougherty

**CONTENT CONSULTANT:**
Captain Charles Weeks
Professor Emeritus in Marine Transportation
Maine Maritime Academy

CAPSTONE PRESS
a capstone imprint

Velocity Books are published by Capstone Press,
1710 Roe Crest Drive, North Mankato, Minnesota 56003
www.capstonepub.com

Copyright © 2015 by Capstone Press, a Capstone imprint. All rights reserved. No part of this publication may be reproduced in whole or in part, or stored in a retrieval system, or transmitted in any form or by any means, electronic, mechanical, photocopying, recording, or otherwise, without written permission of the publisher.

Library of Congress Cataloging-in-Publication Data
Cataloging-in-publication information is on file with the Library of Congress.
ISBN 978-1-4914-0420-1 (library binding)
ISBN 978-1-4914-0424-9 (ebook PDF)

**Editorial Credits**
Lauren Coss, editor; Craig Hinton, designer and production specialist

**Photo Credits**
Alamy: capt digby, 27 (bottom), Mary Evans Picture Library, 9 (right), 23, Presselect, 17 (bottom); Corbis: Splash News, 25 (foreground), 25 (background); Dorling Kindersley, 32, 42; Library of Congress: 31 (bottom), 40, Harris & Ewing, 30, 44; Maritime Quest, 6, 10 (left), 11, 29 (bottom); Newscom: akg-images, 13, Brendan McDermid/Reuters, 34, CB2/ZOB/Wenn.com, 15 (bottom), Emmanuel Dunand/AFP/Getty Images, 26 (bottom), Everett Collection, 41, Roslan Rahman/AFP/Getty Images, 12 (bottom); Nixon Farm, cover; PA Images: Topham Picturepoint, 16–17; Painting © Ken Marschall, 4–5, 28, 33, 35, 39; Red Line Editorial, 36, 37 (bottom), 43; Shutterstock Images: Armin Rose, 15 (top), exopixe, 12 (top), Jane Rix, 45, optimarc, 19 (background); SuperStock: Universal Images Group, 8, 9 (left), 10 (right), 18, 22, 24, 26 (top), 27 (top); State Library of Queensland, 29 (top); Thinkstock: bajinda, 19 (top right), Diana Taliun, 19 (bottom), Dorling Kindersley, 31 (top), 37 (top), payphoto, 19 (top left); Weldon Owen: Barry Croucher/The Art Agency, 14, Peter Bull Art Studio, 7, 20–21, 38

**Artistic Effects**
Shutterstock Images

**Source Notes**
Page 4 • Frederick Fleet, quoted in *Voyagers of the Titanic* by Richard Davenport-Hines. New York: HarperCollins, 2012. Page 206.; Page 7 • Sidney Daniels, quoted in *Titanic Voices* by Donald Hysop, et al. New York: St. Martins Press, 1997. Page 81.; Page 8 • Bruce Ismay, quoted in *Titanic: Legacy of the World's Greatest Ocean Liner*, by Susan Wels. Del Mar, Cal.: Tehabi Books, 1997. Page 17.; Page 26 • *Titanic* telegraph messages, from "Titanic: The Final Messages from a Stricken Ship," by Sean Coughlan, as published by *BBC News* on April 9, 2012. http://www.bbc.com/news/magazine-17631595; Page 29 (top) • *Baltic* telegraph message to *Titanic*, from the British Wreck Commissioner's Inquiry Report, as published on *Titanic Inquiry Project*. http://www.titanicinquiry.org/BOTInq/BOTReport/BOTRepMessages.php; Page 29 (middle) • *Mesaba* telegraph message to *Titanic*, as read by Sir Robert Finlay, from the British Wreck Commissioner's Inquiry Report, as published on *Titanic Inquiry Project*. http://www.titanicinquiry.org/BOTInq/BOTInq32Arguments04.php; Page 29 (bottom) • *Californian* telegraph message to *Titanic*, from the British Wreck Commissioner's Inquiry Report, as published on *Titanic Inquiry Project*. http://www.titanicinquiry.org/BOTInq/BOTReport/botRepCalifornian.php; Page 35 • Joseph Scarrott, quoted in *Titanic Voices* by Donald Hysop, et al. New York: St. Martins Press, 1997. Page 142.; Page 40 (top) • Harold Bride, quoted in *Titanic Voices* by Donald Hysop, et al. New York: St. Martins Press, 1997. Page 152.; Page 40 (bottom) • Jack Podesta, quoted in *Titanic Voices* by Donald Hysop, et al. New York: St. Martins Press, 1997. Page 161.; Page 41 (top) • Charles Herbert Lightoller, quoted in *Titanic Voices* by Donald Hysop, et al. New York: St. Martins Press, 1997. Page 160.; Page 41 (bottom) • George Moore, as quoted in the British Wreck Commissioner's Inquiry Report, as published on *Titanic Inquiry Project*. http://www.titanicinquiry.org/USInq/AmInq07Moore01.php

3 1561 00268 6859

Printed in the United States of America in Stevens Point, Wisconsin.
032014    008092WZF14

# Table of Contents

**INTRODUCTION**
**"Iceberg Right Ahead!"** ............ 4

**CHAPTER 1**
**Assembling the Crew** ............... 6

**CHAPTER 2**
**At Sea** ..................................... 14

**CHAPTER 3**
**All Hands on Deck** .................. 28

**CHAPTER 4**
**Tragedy and Rescue** ............... 36

GLOSSARY ................................. 46

READ MORE ............................... 47

CRITICAL THINKING
USING THE COMMON CORE ....... 47

INTERNET SITES ........................ 47

INDEX ....................................... 48

# "Iceberg Right Ahead!"

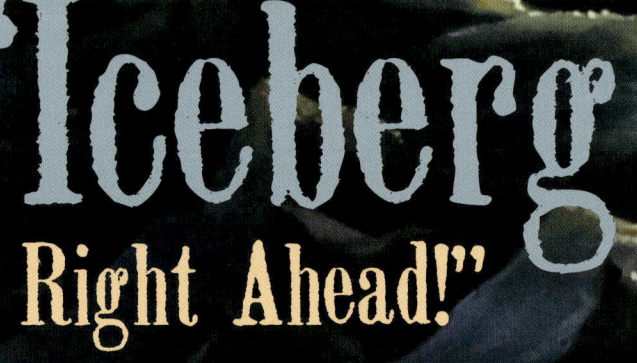

In the **crow's nest** of *Titanic*, **lookouts** Frederick Fleet and Reginald Lee braced against the cold. The ship sped through the night at 22 knots, or 25 miles (40 kilometers) per hour. The two men peered into the darkness for any objects that might lie in *Titanic*'s path. They knew the dark water held many dangers.

As the night wore on, a slight haze came over the ocean. At 11:40 p.m. a large, black object loomed ahead. Fleet quickly rang the warning bell three times and phoned the ship's officers.

"Iceberg right ahead!" Fleet exclaimed.

**crow's nest**—a lookout post located high above a ship
**lookout**—a person who keeps watch for dangers from a high point with a 360° view

*Titanic*'s lookouts were not able to spot the iceberg soon enough to save the ship from destruction.

The officer thanked him. Seconds passed before Fleet saw the ship's **bow** veer to the left. He did not feel the ship hit the iceberg. He was not aware of water spraying into its lower levels. In less than three hours, *Titanic* sank. More than 600 crew members and 800 passengers lost their lives in one of the world's most famous disasters.

**bow**—the front end of a ship

CHAPTER 1

# Assembling the Crew

*Titanic was designed to be the most luxurious ship of its time.*

## Chance of a Lifetime

The massive *Titanic* attracted attention even before its **maiden** voyage ended in tragedy on April 15, 1912. At the time, it was the largest ship in the world. The ship's designers also wanted to make it the most luxurious. Many of *Titanic*'s cabins were as elegant as fine hotel rooms. The ship included a swimming pool, a gym, and four elevators. People thought *Titanic* was almost unsinkable because some lower compartments had watertight doors the crew could close in an emergency.

**FACT:** There were 885 crew members on *Titanic*, plus eight musicians and five postal clerks.

Crew members loaded up the ship with the goods it would need on its journey across the Atlantic.

> 66 [I felt] as many others did—proud to be selected for such a wonderful ship. 99
>
> —Sidney Daniels, *third-class steward*

Crew members were eager to work on *Titanic*. When the White Star Line made jobs available, hundreds of workers quickly signed on. Most of the ship's seamen, stewards, and **boiler** room workers were British, but other crew members came from all over the world. Waiters and chefs were from Italy, France, and Switzerland. Some postal workers came from the United States.

When crew members boarded the ship on April 10, 1912, in Southampton, England, they expected to work hard. It would not be easy to keep the 883-foot (269-meter) ship running smoothly and take care of its 1,317 passengers. However, crew members felt honored. White Star Line chose only the best crew members to be part of *Titanic*'s first journey across the Atlantic.

**maiden**—first

**boiler**—a device that creates steam to power a ship's engine

# The Millionaire's Captain

The popular Captain Edward Smith was in charge of *Titanic*. Smith was well liked by passengers. So many rich passengers traveled aboard his ships that he was known as the Millionaire's Captain. He had worked at sea for nearly 40 years and was now Senior Master of the White Star fleet.

Smith had a reputation for keeping his ships safe. "He was a man in whom we had entire and absolute confidence," said Bruce Ismay, the chairman of the White Star Line.

A crew of seven officers worked under the captain. They made sure the ship was in good working order as the captain prepared to sail. They also made sure the ship stayed on course while at sea.

Captain Edward Smith was 62 years old when he died on the *Titanic*.

First Officer William Murdoch

Fifth Officer Harold Lowe

## Titanic's Officers

| Title | Name | Age | Years at Sea |
|---|---|---|---|
| CHIEF OFFICER | Henry Wilde | 39 | 25 |
| FIRST OFFICER | William Murdoch | 39 | 25 |
| SECOND OFFICER | Charles Herbert Lightoller | 38 | 24 |
| THIRD OFFICER | Herbert Pitman | 34 | 17 |
| FOURTH OFFICER | Joseph Boxhall | 28 | 13 |
| FIFTH OFFICER | Harold Lowe | 28 | 14 |
| SIXTH OFFICER | James Moody | 24 | 10 |

# On Deck

A number of crew members helped the captain and officers keep the ship running smoothly.

## TITANIC'S CHAIN OF COMMAND

**CAPTAIN**
Commanded *Titanic*, including determining speed and setting a course

**OFFICERS**
Executed the captain's orders; led the ship's navigation; patrolled the ship to make sure everything was in order and working properly; kept captain up-to-date on ship's day-to-day operations

**CHIEF PURSER**
Took care of money and other valuables on the ship

**QUARTERMASTER**
Steered the ship and helped officers keep it on course; relayed orders from officers to other crew members

Second Officer Charles Herbert Lightoller

Hugh McElroy was *Titanic's* chief purser.

**BOATSWAIN**
In charge of the able seamen and helped them with their duties

**ABLE SEAMEN**
Raised the ship's anchors and tied up the ship when in port; stowed **cargo**; painted, repaired, and cleaned the ship

**ASSISTANT PURSER**
Worked in the purser's office; waited on passengers who wanted to send a telegram, buy a ticket for the ship's swimming pool, or store valuable items

**SEAMEN**
Less experienced than able seamen; helped keep the ship in good repair

Captain Smith and other crew members peer over *Titanic*'s edge as it prepares for its maiden voyage.

## LUCKY TO BE LATE

Three brothers, Alfred, Bertram, and Thomas Slade, just missed getting onboard *Titanic*. They planned to work in the ship's boiler room and arrived just as the boarding platform was about to be pulled back. The officer in charge would not let them on board. Other men had filled their jobs. The brothers lost their chance to work on *Titanic*. But being late may have saved their lives. Only 22 percent of the men working in the boiler room survived.

**cargo**—the goods carried by a ship, vehicle, or aircraft

# Rounding out the Crew

*Titanic*'s crew included a variety of workers in addition to the captain, officers, and other sailors. Stewards and stewardesses cared for passengers, while cooks and bakers prepared meals. Firemen **stoked** the boilers that powered the ship's engines, and engineers kept the machinery running.

## Odd Jobs

Some crew members had unusual duties or job titles.

**BUGLER:** Played a tune to alert passengers to mealtimes

**BOOTS STEWARDS:** Polished shoes and boots

**GREASERS:** Oiled, cleaned, and fixed engines

**LIFT OPERATORS:** Ran the ship's elevators

**BUTTONS:** Ran errands for guests and crew members

Boots stewards may have polished shoes like these that were recovered from *Titanic*'s wreck at the bottom of the ocean.

stoke—to stir or add fuel to something that is burning

A bugle is a musical instrument similar to a trumpet.

Specific crew members operated *Titanic*'s three first-class elevators and one second-class elevator.

**FACT:** Twenty-three female crew members worked aboard *Titanic*. They included 21 stewardesses and two restaurant cashiers.

## Chapter 2
# At Sea

## On the Bridge

As *Titanic* headed across the Atlantic Ocean, the captain, officers, and other sailors took their places on the **bridge** at the top of the ship. The quartermaster steered the ship from the wheelhouse at the back of the bridge. Crew members in the center of the bridge watched the ship's speed and direction. When it was time to speed up or slow down, they sent orders to the engine room. Officers used telephones at the back of the wheelhouse to call engineers in the engine room. They also used signal dials to communicate speed changes to the engine room. An officer moved the bridge signal dial, which caused a dial in the engine room to point to the speed the officer wanted. Behind the wheelhouse was the chart room, where officers tracked the ship's course. They posted weather reports and messages about ice there as well.

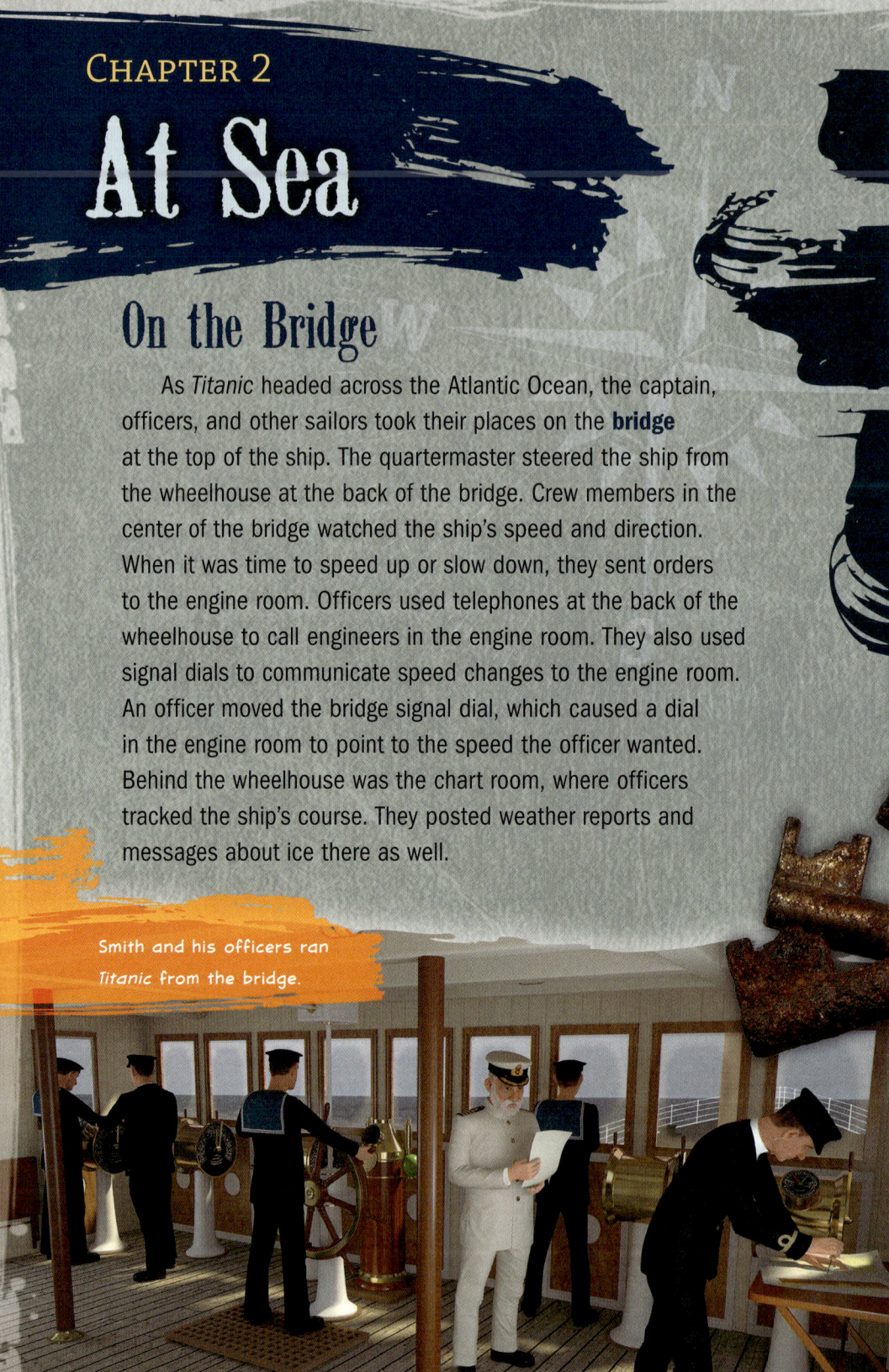

Smith and his officers ran *Titanic* from the bridge.